Zen Ghosts

BY JON J MUTH

SCHOLASTIC INC.

CALGARY PUBLIC LIBRARY

AUG   2017

Copyright © 2010 by Jon J Muth

All rights reserved. Published by Scholastic Inc. SCHOLASTIC and associated
logos are trademarks and/or registered trademarks of Scholastic Inc.

No part of this publication may be reproduced, stored in a retrieval system,
or transmitted in any form or by any means, electronic, mechanical,
photocopying, recording, or otherwise, without written permission of the
publisher. For information regarding permission, write to Scholastic Inc.,
Attention: Permissions Department, 557 Broadway, New York, NY 10012.

This book was originally published in hardcover by Scholastic Press in 2010.

ISBN 978-0-545-47133-6

LIBRARY OF CONGRESS CATALOGING-IN-PUBLICATION
DATA AVAILABLE

12 11 10 9 8 7 6 5 4 3 2 1   12 13 14 15 16/0

Printed in China   95

This edition first printing, July 2012

The text was set in Monotype Fournier.

Jon Muth's artwork was created with watercolor and ink.

Book design by David Saylor

ACKNOWLEDGMENTS

I am deeply grateful to my wife, Bonnie, for her
inexhaustible capacity to start again; to Dianne Hess
for her good faith, trust, humor, and patience; to Allen
Spiegel for being my partner and friend; to David Saylor
for stopping time so I could make this book the way
you see it now; to Ryushin for life-changing assistance;
to Stephen Andreski for our walks into the wilderness
of the self; and to my children, whose sometimes silent,
sometimes unruly example has been my constant teacher.

For John Daido Loori, Roshi

(1931–2009)

Zen Teacher and Abbot of Zen Mountain Monastery

. . . *thank you.*

"MICHAEL! There's a ghost outside!" said Karl.
"A what?" asked Michael.

"A big, scary-looking ghost!" said Karl.

"Is it Stillwater?" asked Michael.

"It doesn't have Stillwater's face," said Karl. "Oh, wait.
Yes, he does! Come in, Stillwater!"

"Hi, Stillwater!" said Addy. "Happy almost Halloween! We are working on our costumes. I'm going to be a Moon Princess. What are you going to be?"

"I'm a ghost," said Stillwater. "What are you going to be?" he asked Karl and Michael.

"I'm going to be a monster," said Karl, "with a powerful heat ray and atomic breath! I will cause awesome destruction!"

"I haven't decided what I'm going to be yet," said Michael. "Either an owl . . . or a pirate. I really like owls and I really like pirates."

"Perhaps you will be an Owl-Pirate," said Stillwater.

"He can't be an Owl-Pirate!" said Karl. "There's no such thing as an Owl-Pirate! He has to be *one* thing."

"He can be whatever he wants!" said Addy.
"Look, Stillwater! Do you like my costume?"

"Yes," said Stillwater. "It reminds me of something. This is a very special Halloween. There is going to be a full moon and I know someone who will tell you a ghost story."

"Yay!" said Addy.

"I love ghosts stories!" said Michael.

"It's not too scary, is it?" asked Karl.

"After trick-or-treating, meet me by the big stone wall
and I will take you to the storyteller," said Stillwater.

When the children were done trick or treating, they waited by the stone wall.

"I'll trade you three Tiny Mints for one Snookers!" said Addy.

"No!" said Karl. "I'm not giving up my Snookers!"

"But you don't even like them!" said Addy. "Come on!"

"I only like Tiny Mints if they are the Crunch Peppermint kind," said Karl. "Besides, I am saving my Snookers. I have one flavored like bam—"

"BOO!" said Stillwater.

"Wow! You scared me!" said Karl. "How long have you been there?"

"Follow me!" said Stillwater.

"I've never gone this way before," said Michael.

"Me, neither," said Karl.

"I think I have," said Addy.

In a few moments, they arrived at Stillwater's house.

"It is very misty," said Addy.

"Come in," said Stillwater.

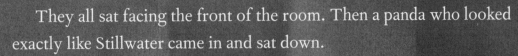

They all sat facing the front of the room. Then a panda who looked exactly like Stillwater came in and sat down.

"Is that Stillwater?" whispered Karl.

"Yes . . . no! . . . I don't know! Shhh!" whispered Michael.

The panda held up a brush and said, "I am going to draw you a story. . . ."

ONCE, A LONG, LONG TIME AGO, there was a young girl named Senjo. Her parents loved her very much, and they took very good care of her.

She had a best friend named Ochu, whom she had known for as long as she could remember. They were together so much that Senjo's father would laugh and say, "You two are so well-matched, you will probably end up marrying each other!"

As they grew up, they believed this would happen, and they fell in love.

But when Senjo reached marrying age, her father suddenly became ill and couldn't work.

He came to her one evening and told her that she was to wed a nice man named Henryo. Henryo was prosperous and could take care of the family.

Now Senjo was very sad. She had always hoped she would marry her best friend, Ochu.

When Ochu heard about this, he decided to leave that very night. He couldn't stand to be in the same village where his beloved Senjo would be married to someone else. At midnight, with a full moon, he secretly went to the river's edge, packed his boat, and left. He didn't tell anyone — not even Senjo.

As he traveled up the river, he saw a vague figure running along the bank. His heart leapt when he saw that it was Senjo, and he hurried to her side. They hugged each other tightly and decided to go off together.

Senjo and Ochu journeyed to a faraway
village where they married and had two children.
They were very happy.

Then one day Senjo came to Ochu in tears.
She longed to be with her parents and to see
her home again. Ochu felt the same way.
They decided to return together and face the
consequences.

When they arrived at the dock, Ochu said, "Let me go first to see your father. I will apologize and find out how things are before you come."

Senjo's father was very happy to see him. Ochu told him they were sorry for what they had done, and that he and Senjo were now a family with two children.

Senjo's father was astonished. "What are you talking about?" he asked. "From the time you left the village, Senjo has been very sick in bed. She is unable to speak!"

Now Ochu was surprised. "But I promise you, Senjo is well — and you are a grandfather! I will bring her to you."

As Ochu went to the dock, Senjo's father rushed to his daughter's bedside and told her what Ochu had said. As she heard the story, she was filled with joy. Without saying a word, she rose from her bed and went quickly down the stairs.

At that very moment, the Senjo who had come ashore arrived at the house with Ochu. The two Senjos, upon seeing each other, merged and became one.

The storyteller paused, then he asked, "Which Senjo is the true one? Are they one or are they two?"

Addy, Michael, and Karl looked at one another.
Then they turned and looked beside them. Only a
mask was sitting on the cushion.

They looked at Stillwater sitting in the front of the room. He was reaching into a bag of Halloween candy. "I got a bunch of Wizzles and Tiny Mints. Does anyone have some bamboo-flavored Snookers?"

"I've been saving one for you!" said Karl.

"Thank you," said Stillwater.

"Thank *you*," said Karl. "That was a good story."

Author's Note

THE STORY *Senjo and Her Soul Are Separated* was first told to me by John Daido Loori, Roshi. It was originally written down by Master Wu-men Hui-hai (1183–1260), a Chinese Buddhist monk, and appears in his collection of forty-eight koans called *The Gateless Gate*. Master Wu-men's book, along with *The Blue Cliff Record*, which contains one hundred koans, are what Zen students sometimes contemplate in their efforts for enlightenment.

Senjo's name and the title of the story vary in different translations. *Quinnu Parted from Her Higher Soul* and *Seijo's Separated Soul* are just two of the many other versions.

Koans are basically questions that you have to answer for yourself. They appeal directly to the intuitive part of human consciousness, not to the intellect. You can't think them through. You can't intellectualize them. You can, but you will miss the point.

Foremost, Senjo's story is simply a great ghost story. It raises the hair on the back of my neck whenever I hear it. It is the kind of story that leaves you with more questions than it answers. Stories like that can't be neatly wrapped up and placed on a quiet shelf and forgotten. The thoughts they raise are constantly reemerging and changing as we go through our lives.

In your hands is the story I took away from hearing three different Zen monks tell it. Originally, I heard it from Zen Master Daido Loori, Roshi. Then with gratitude to Geoffrey Shugen Arnold, Sensei, and Konrad Ryushin Marchaj, Sensei, my understanding of the tale grew until it became *Zen Ghosts*. It's not an abstract, historic event that happened 1,000 years ago. It's very much about you and me today.

I wanted to offer this story to children because at a very young age we discover questions about duality. There is the *me* I am with my parents, the *me* I am with my friends, and there is still another *me* with a different group of my friends. I am my mother's son when I am with her, but am I not also my mother's son when I am with my friends? Do I act differently? What if they want me to do something my mother's son would not do? Am I being dishonest with someone? With myself? When our hearts are taken in two different directions, where are we? This particular koan happens to be a very old Chinese story, but it is a story that happens every day in our lives.

Koans don't have right or wrong answers as much as they have responses that show understanding. In Zen Buddhism, the teacher who gives you a koan is looking to see if you truly have digested the question. And if you have, the answer becomes your own.